Clive the Hamster

COLLINGWOOD O'HARE ENTERTAINMENT LTD
Created by Trevor Ricketts and Christopher O'Hare
Series developed by Tony Collingwood
Copyright © 2001 by Collingwood O'Hare Entertainment Ltd.

First published in Great Britain in 2001 by HarperCollins*Children's Books*,
a division of HarperCollins*Publishers* Ltd,
77-85 Fulham Palace Road, Hammersmith, London W6 8JB.
ISBN: 0 00 710871 0
1 3 5 7 9 10 8 6 4 2

The HarperCollins website address is:
www.**fire**and**water**.com

Printed and bound in Hong Kong

ANIMAL
STORIES

Clive the Hamster

Written by Alan Gilbey

An imprint of HarperCollins*Publishers*

There once was a Hamster
Who answered to Clive.
But he, to be honest,
Of all creatures alive...

Wasn't the nicest
Or sweetest of fellas.
In fact, he was mean,
And terribly jealous.

When he saw a big cake
With a very small Rabbit,
Clive licked his lips
And said, "I must have it!

Ooh! That looks tasty!
Ooh! That looks sweet!"
So Clive scared the Rabbit,
Who beat a retreat.

Making sure that the candles
Were all blown out first,
Clive stuffed in the cake
Till his cheeks nearly burst.

When the Rabbit returned,
He looked round and round.
He looked behind Clive,
Then he looked on the ground.

"Where is my cake?
Where can it be?"
Clive shrugged his shoulders –
"Don't look at me!"

Then he turned on his tail,
And went off in a huff.
He would have gone home,
But cake wasn't enough.

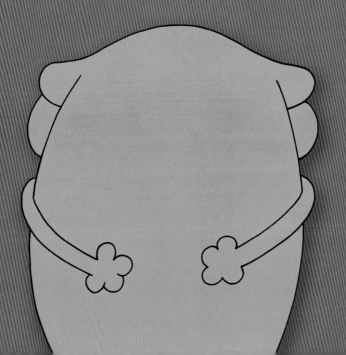

Then he saw Doris
Choosing hats at a stall.
They were all shapes and sizes –
Tall, short, big and small.

"Ooh! They look tasty!
Ooh! I'd look cool,
If I had that head wear
And wore it to school!"

So Clive scared poor Doris
And frightened her off.
Then he snatched up the hats
And had a quick scoff.

When Doris returned,
She looked round and round.
She looked behind Clive,
Then she looked on the ground.

"Where are my hats?
Where can they be?"
Clive shrugged his shoulders –
"Don't look at me!"

Clive would have gone home,
Had he not heard the sound,
Of some kind of music
Sh-sh-shaking the ground.

And he spotted a Gerbil,
Whose name was Young Dean,
With a bass-boosted-boom-box
Type, music machine.

"Ooh! That looks tasty!
Ooh! That looks neat."
So Clive scared the Gerbil
Who beat a retreat.

When the Gerbil returned,
He looked round and round.
He looked behind Clive,
Then he looked on the ground.

"Hey, where's my music?
Where can it be?"
Clive shrugged his shoulders –
"Don't look at me!"

Then the music machine
Played the next song,
And its beat was so bumpy
Clive's head thumped along!

"Help me!" squealed Clive,
But the sound was too loud.
The Gerbil was singing
And dancing around.

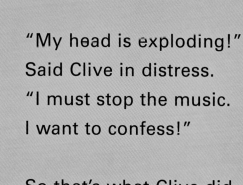

"My head is exploding!"
Said Clive in distress.
"I must stop the music.
I want to confess!"

So that's what Clive did.
He emptied his cheeks,
And out tumbled things
They'd been missing for weeks.

Doris said, "Clive,
All this stealing and stealth,
Has not really hurt us.
You stole from yourself!

This cake, and those hats,
And that tape machine too,
Were part of a party
We were planning for you!"

Clive saw he'd been selfish,
While they'd all been caring.
"Instead of my stealing,
I could have been sharing."

He said he was sorry,
And was good all that week.
So they still threw a party,
And played hide and seek.

The Rabbit hid first.
Where could he be?
Clive shrugged his shoulders –
"Don't look at me!"

The End